THE YAWNS ARE COMING!

CHRISTOPHER ELIOPOULOS

 DIAL BOOKS FOR YOUNG READERS

For Audra

DIAL BOOKS FOR YOUNG READERS
An imprint of Penguin Random House LLC, New York

Copyright © 2020 by Christopher Eliopoulos

Visit us at penguinrandomhouse.com

Library of Congress Cataloging-in-Publication Data is available.
ISBN 9781984816306 • Printed in China • 10 9 8 7 6 5 4 3 2 1

Designed by Jason Henry • Text set in Avenir
The artwork for this book was created digitally.

We were going to have **so much fun!**

My best friend, Noodles, was at my house for a sleepover.
But we weren't going to sleep.
We were planning to stay up all

night

long.

We made a list of all the fun things we would do.

We played hide-and-seek,

and board games,

and soccer.

We jumped on the trampoline.

And when it got dark, we collected fireflies.

Then it happened.

There were hundreds of them.

We ran.

And we climbed.

And we sneaked.

And we hid.

But it was no use.

The **YAWNS** caught us!

We couldn't resist them.

I would

Then Noodles would

But I wasn't having it.

Then I would

again.

Then Noodles would

again.

Then, out of nowhere...

SPLAP!

A **DOZE** landed on Noodles' head.

I tried to keep Noodles awake.
We still had lots of items on our list of fun things to do.

But it was too late.

The **SNORES** had arrived and were dancing around Noodles' head.

My eyes were getting heavy.

They were just about to close when...

A **SLEEPIE** covered me up.

It was warm and safe.

Before I knew it . . .

It was morning.

Noodles, who was awake and smiling, had made a new list.

We were going to have **so much fun!**